Dear Parent:

Congratulations! Your child is taking the first steps on an exciting journey. The destination? Independent reading!

STEP INTO READING® will help your child get there. The program offers five steps to reading success. Each step includes fun stories and colorful art. There are also Step into Reading Sticker Books, Step into Reading Math Readers, Step into Reading Phonics Readers, Step into Reading Write-In Readers, and Step into Reading Phonics Boxed Sets—a complete literacy program with something to interest every child.

Learning to Read, Step by Step!

Ready to Read   Preschool–Kindergarten
• big type and easy words • rhyme and rhythm • picture clues
For children who know the alphabet and are eager to begin reading.

Reading with Help   Preschool–Grade 1
• basic vocabulary • short sentences • simple stories
For children who recognize familiar words and sound out new words with help.

Reading on Your Own   Grades 1–3
• engaging characters • easy-to-follow plots • popular topics
For children who are ready to read on their own.

Reading Paragraphs   Grades 2–3
• challenging vocabulary • short paragraphs • exciting stories
For newly independent readers who read simple sentences with confidence.

Ready for Chapters   Grades 2–4
• chapters • longer paragraphs • full-color art
For children who want to take the plunge into chapter books but still like colorful pictures.

STEP INTO READING® is designed to give every child a successful reading experience. The grade levels are only guides. Children can progress through the steps at their own speed, developing confidence in their reading, no matter what their grade.

Remember, a lifetime love of reading starts with a single step!

Visit us on the Web!
StepIntoReading.com
www.randomhouse.com/kids
Educators and librarians, for a variety of teaching tools, visit us at
www.randomhouse.com/teachers

Library of Congress Cataloging-in-Publication Data
Lagonegro, Melissa.
Kingdom of color / by Melissa Lagonegro ; illustrated by Jean-Paul Orpiñas, Elena Naggi, and
Studio IBOIX.
p. cm. — (Step into reading. Step 1)
ISBN 978-0-7364-2687-9 (trade) — ISBN 978-0-7364-8084-0 (lib. bdg.)
I. Orpiñas, Jean-Paul. II. Naggi, Elena. III. Iboix Estudi. IV. Tangled (Motion picture). V. Title.
PZ8.L1362Ki 2010 398.2—dc22 [E] 2009053397

Printed in the United States of America   20 19 18 17 16 15

Kingdom of Color

By Melissa Lagonegro

Illustrated by Jean-Paul Orpiñas,
Elena Naggi, and Studio IBOIX

Random House 🏠 New York

Rapunzel lives
in a tower.
She sees lights
and colors.

Rapunzel painted
the walls.
She used many colors.

Pascal is

Rapunzel's friend.

He changes color.

Rapunzel wants to see
more colors.
Flynn Rider
will help.

Green grass and leaves.

Red flowers.

Gray bunny.

Flynn and Rapunzel

are surprised!

Rapunzel wears

a purple dress.

Long yellow hair.

White horse.

Brown saddle.

Black hoof.

Big blue sky.

23

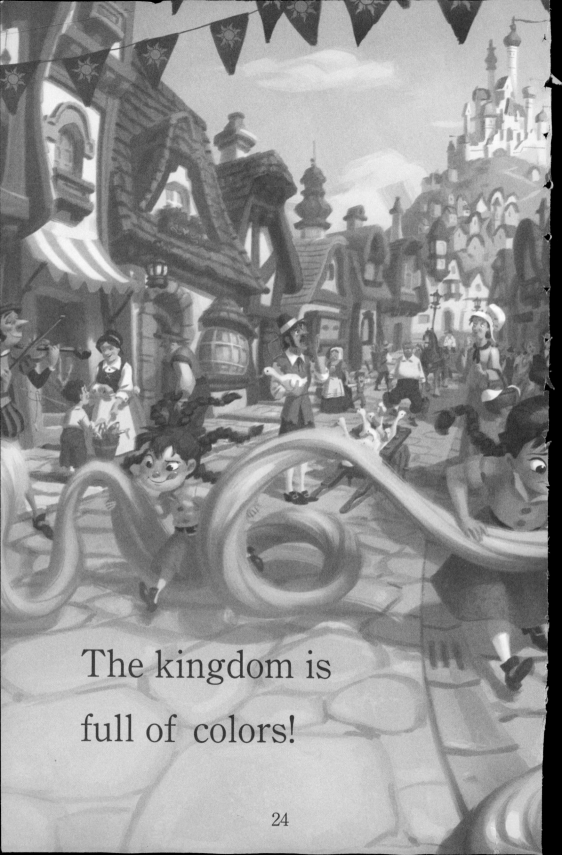

The kingdom is
full of colors!

Rapunzel finds
a pretty picture.

She sees the colors
blue, yellow, purple,
red, green, and brown.

Rapunzel and Flynn
have so much fun!

Rapunzel sees the lights
up close!
They make the sky bright.

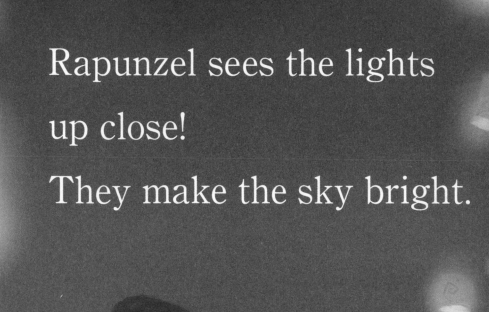

Rapunzel is happy.

She loves colors.

She loves the lights.